ISIS:
WRATH OF THE CYBERGODDESS

Also by Shawn James

ISIS

Isis: Trial of the Goddess

Isis: Amari's Revenge

Isis: The Ultimate Fight

Isis: The Beauty Myth

Isis: Death of a Theta

Isis: My Sister, My Frenemy

Isis: All About the Goddess

The Cassandra Cookbook

All About Marilyn

The Temptation of John Haynes

All About Nikki- The Fabulous First Season

If you have questions and comments about this book send your E-mails to Shawn James at:

sjsdirectny@aol.com

And check out Shawn James' blog at:

shawnsjames.blogspot.com

ISIS:
WRATH OF THE CYBERGODDESS

SHAWN JAMES

That page with the legal stuff on it

Copyrights © 2014 Shawn James. All Rights Reserved.

Isis: Wrath of the Cybergoddess ISBN-13: 978-1495352362
ISBN-10: 1495352366

Published by SJS DIRECT, Bronx, NY 10456. No part of this book may be reproduced or transmitted in any form or by any means, graphic, electronic, or mechanical, including photocopying, recording, taping or by any information storage or retrieval system, without the permission in writing from the publisher.

Original front cover art by Bill Walko.

This is a work of fiction. All events, locations, institutions, themes, persons, characters and plot are completely fictional. Any resemblance to places or person, living or deceased, are purely coincidental.

Dedicated to my inspiration and my muse.

Acknowledgments

I would like to thank God for helping me write this book. If not for Him, I would have never finished this story. With His help maybe I'll be able to take my craft to the next level.

I'd also like to thank my Mother for supporting me and my writing career all these years.

A special thanks to my brother Steve for inspiring me and giving me hope during some of the hardest times of my life.

A special thanks to artist Bill Walko for taking the time to design the awesome cover for this book.

I'd also like to thank my sister Shawna for giving me a copy of Syd Field's *Screenplay*. That book helped me learn the basics about screenwriting and helped me learn a whole new set of writing skills.

In addition, I'd like to thank fellow writers Liz Issacs, Savannah North and Francine Craft for their continued support and advice that helped me further develop my writing craft.

Finally, I'd like to thank my POD printer. If not for this great technology, this story would be sitting at the bottom of a closet forgotten for years to come.

WRATH OF THE CYBERGODDESS

Chapter 1

There is no God. And there definitely isn't a goddess.

There's clearly a scientific explanation for everything that Isis woman did in my lab a few months ago. The so-called teleporting, the displays of incredible strength, invulnerability, and even the flying. If she's flesh and blood like I am there has to be a biological way to not only restore my lost youth, but replicate those amazing abilities.

Ever since I got out of the hospital, I've been working day and night to break the biological barrier between humans and these alleged gods. After three months of research I think I've finally made my scientific breakthrough. If the computer models I designed for this nanocell are correct, it should re-write my DNA reconstructing my 85-year-old body back into something resembling myself in my twenties.

I'm taking one last look at the codes on the nanocell in the digital electron microscope when the intercom beeps. What do I pay those fools at the security desk for! I told them I was not to be disturbed when I was in the lab! I huff a sigh, storm over to the intercom on the wall near the lab doors and hit talk.

"Oh, what is it?" I bark.

"Miss Sanders, I hate to interrupt you, but your niece Ramona is here to see you." the guard says.

I thought I told her to take care of my business affairs in New York. "Tell her I'm busy-"

"She says it's urgent."

It's always urgent with her. "Oh, send her in." I snarl pressing the button to unlock the titanium security doors.

As the titanium doors begin sliding back, I storm back over to the table where my work is and take one last look at the nanocell. After I confirm that the biocodes for the DNA re-sequencing program are correct, I take the slide off the microscope and place the cell into a Petri dish filled with my blood. Before I can fill a syringe with the nanocell, I hear the clop of Ramona's Italian high heels pounding into the tiled floors. When the tall bronze colored woman dressed in a tailored black Italian business suit storms through the white swinging doors I greet the reflection of her scowl in my monitor with a pasted on smile.

"Good Afternoon Ramona. What can I do for you?"

"Auntie, what are you trying to do bankrupt this company?" Ramona barks.

Figures. She's worried about her inheritance. "It's not your money yet." I dismiss. "I can spend it however I wish."

"You just spent over twelve million dollars on a supercomputer. What do we need with a supercomputer?"

"I can't program a nanobot with a laptop."

"Nanobot? How does that relate to our business-"

"It relates to *my* business."

"Auntie, I can't keep explaining these crazy expenditures of yours to the board or to our investors. They're asking questions-"

"So tell them it's all for research-"

WRATH OF THE CYBERGODDESS

"Research on what? These crazy mad scientist experiments of yours?"

How dare she question my work. "It's not a mad scientist experiment Ramona. It's a mission to take humanity on the next step up the evolutionary ladder."

"Evolutionary ladder?" Ramona huffs. "Are you listening to yourself? We sell cosmetics-"

"We sell whatever I want to sell."

"Well, we're not going to be able to pay for anything if you keep burning through our money like this. I'm barely going to have enough money for this week's payroll let alone offer a settlement to that woman you kidnapped a few months ago-"

"I told you she's not a woman!" I bark. "She's not human-"

"She's human enough to sue us!" Ramona snarls back.

"You saw the security video, you saw what she did-"

"I saw a woman you kidnapped and assaulted defending herself from your plans to murder her. You're lucky she hasn't pressed charges-"

She's probably afraid I'll reveal her secret. That's why she hasn't followed up with law enforcement or legal action. "And I guess you're trying to protect us from her lawsuit."

"Someone has to look out for your best interests-"

"I ought to fire you."

"Look Auntie, I've humored you and these little experiments of yours ever since you got out of the hospital. But now you're hurting other people-"

I catch the desperate look in her eyes in the reflection of my computer monitor. She thinks I'm old. She thinks I'm senile. She wants to put me in a home. I've got to convince her that what I'm doing is for the greater good. "Ramona, my work isn't done-"

"Auntie, I don't want to have to get a court order-"

My hands clench into fists on hearing her threat. I'd love to throttle the life out of her. "You go get your court order. I'll have my lawyers ready for you when you get back."

Chapter 2

Ramona huffs a sigh as she storms out of my lab. I don't have much time; I need to get this experiment going before she comes back here with that court order. After she shows a judge evidence of my expenditures and scientific theories they'll definitely declare me mentally incompetent. If that happens all the work I've done to restore my youth and become the next step in human evolution will be for nothing.

I hurry over to the Petri dish where my nanocell is floating. I fill my syringe, roll up the sleeve of my blouse, find a vein and grit my teeth as I prick my arm with the needle and inject it into my bloodstream. If I wrote that code right the nanocells should start replicating immediately when introduced to the body.

The fast acting nanocells catch me by surprise; I feel my body tingling as they begin working inside me. My heart pounds faster and faster; I feel a numbness in my right arm then my heartbeats start to become erratic. I gasp for breath as I clutch my chest and collapse to the floor. I was so close, so close…

Chapter 3

Everything is so dark. So quiet. So cold. This can't be the so-called afterlife. And it definitely isn't the morgue. I hear the hum of my central air conditioning unit buzzing above me.

Obviously I'm not dead. But everything I see is black except for two words in red: RECONFIGURATION COMPLETE. Could the nanocells have worked? Could they have reconstructed my body? Or have I just given myself a stroke?

Of course they worked, it's the only explanation for why I'm still alive and this prompt is showing up in front of my face. If I wrote this code correctly, all I have to do is access the interface menu to activate the nanocells that make up my new body. With a thought I click out of the reconfiguration prompt and my eyes flutter open. The world is clear as a High-definition television screen as my new eyes peer up at the ceiling of my lab.

I'm surprised at how fast I've become when I spring up off the floor. When I try to lean on the bioscanner's table the steel and glass structure starts to crack in my grasp. Clearly I'm a lot faster and stronger than I was in my prime. I have to wonder if in addition to my newfound abilities if my youth was restored.

I'm eager to see what I look like. I hurry over to the mirror on the far side of the lab. A proud smile grows on my face when I

WRATH OF THE CYBERGODDESS

see the reflection of my beautiful 22-year-old self staring back at me. Unfortunately, my eyes are red, my skin is ice blue, and the silken hair flowing down my back is jet black.

It's nothing I can't fix with a simple palate swap. I hurry over to the computer terminal to access my old *Ebony Fashion Fair* photos. Before I can reach to tap the screen, the folder pops up on it. Here's something interesting; all I have to do is think and I can interface with the computers in the lab. I'll see if I can access the Internet once I get my correct skin tone uploaded to this new body.

I scroll down and find a photo of myself strutting down the runway of the *Ebony Fashion Fair* and bring it up on the screen. I start to feel as fabulous as I did on the runway in the 1950's when I see my hands changing to the caramel color they were years ago. I'm back!

And it's clear from the reconfiguration I'm better than I was before. Perfect. Ready to strut my stuff in this new modern world. I bring up the Sepia computer network with a thought and then bring up Google Chrome on a second monitor to my left. While I scan the video cameras of our Madison Avenue store and study the daily sales receipts, I access over one hundred websites all at once in less than a tenth of a second.

In the distance, I hear footsteps approaching the lab. I bring up the security camera in the hall and see one of the guards who works at the front desk approaching. My eyes grow wide catching the time on the clock in the corner of my eye. 7:45 AM Friday! No wonder she's coming to check on me. I must have been unconscious all day!

I can't risk being discovered looking like this. Since the nanocells in this body have a high iron content, I might be able to fly by reversing the polarity of my body in the opposite direction of the gravitational fields around me. With a thought I change the direction the electrons in my nervous system are flowing so that they repel me from the ground instead of sticking me to it. In a few moments my feet start to rise off the floor. When I ascend into the tall ceilings of the lab, I quickly change my color palate to blend in with my surroundings as the guard pushes past the swinging doors.

"Miss Sanders are you *still* here?" she calls. "I saw the light on-"

As the guard walks further into the lab to investigate, I descend and slip through the swinging doors. My palate swapping ability seems to work well at camouflaging my presence; I can't see myself on any of the hallway security cameras I'm monitoring in a minimized window in the corner of my eye. While I push past the tall glass doors and make my way out to the driveway, the guard in the lab gasps at the sight of my blood on the floor and rushes to the phone to call 911. While I'm eager to go and find that alleged goddess, I think I'll stick around to witness poor Ramona's reaction to my disappearance. Depending on how she responds I may or may not let her keep her inheritance.

Chapter 4

I'm in the shower humming a happy tune when I hear the chirp of my iPhone in the bedroom. As I'm positioning the showerhead to rinse soap off my body, I hear the buzz of the intercom too. I love how everyone always waits until you're in middle of a shower to get in touch with you.

Let's see…who do I want to talk to first? The caller on the phone or the doorman? I ponder the answer to that question while I wrap a towel around myself, streak out of the bathroom, and grab my iPhone off the night table. As a trail of wet footprints march down the hall into the kitchenette, I smile catching Edna's picture on the screen as I cock the intercom receiver to my ear. "Who is it Mike?" I inquire.

"A Ramona Sanders from Sepia Cosmetics to see you Isis."

Ramona Sanders? What's she want to do with me? I guess I won't find out until she comes up. "Send her up." I tell him.

After I hang up the intercom, I hit talk and cock my iPhone to my ear. "Casa de goddess. What's up Doc?"

"Hey Princess, are we still on for lunch at Savoy this afternoon?" Edna inquires.

Definitely. I've been waiting years to see baby Colleen all grown up."

"Wonderful. Colleen can't wait to see you."

I can't wait to see her. I'm hoping our relationship can be just as amicable as the one I had with her parents back in the day. "Did you tell her about me?"

"I told her you were a promising young Theta she should take the time to talk to."

"So I'm still Andrea's great niece."

"That's the official story. Unless you want to pull out the tiara…"

"I'll save the royal attire for a special occasion Doc. Jeans and a blouse will be fine for lunch this afternoon."

"See you then." Edna says hanging up.

I'm about to rush back into the bedroom to get my bathrobe when the doorbell rings. As much as I'd like to preserve my modesty, it'd be ruder to leave a guest waiting. I hurry over to the front door and greet the staid bronze colored woman dressed in a tailored Italian business suit and heels with a smile when I crack it open. "Isis?" Ramona greets extending her hand.

"That's me." I reply shaking it.

"Ramona Sanders, Vice President and Chief Operating Officer of Sepia Cosmetics. I wanted to talk to you about the incident at our store and our Alexandria laboratory a few months ago."

Incident. She says that with such indifference that it sends a chill down my spine. But she has to care if she come out here herself and speak to me face-to-face. Usually these corporate types like to send their high-priced lawyers to deal with small stuff like this.

"Why don't you come in?" I say gesturing to my sofa. "You can have a seat."

WRATH OF THE CYBERGODDESS

On the invite, Ramona strolls into the living room, has a seat on the sofa and puts her briefcase on my coffee table. As I ease into the cushion across from her, she gives me an awkward look. "Don't you want to get dressed?" She asks.

I'd love to rush down the hall to get my robe, but I don't know her like that to leave her in any part of my apartment alone for even a short period of time. It'd be better if we just took care of business. "You're not seeing anything you haven't seen in the video." I retort.

"I offer you my sincerest apologies about the ordeal you went through at our store and our Alexandria facility."

"It's okay."

"It's not okay with me. I'd like to settle this matter in a way that fairly compensates you for your pain and suffering."

"I thought the matter was settled when you didn't decline my online order last month."

"I think we can do better than a gift card." Ramona continues. "Can I ask why didn't you pursue legal action against us?"

I didn't want to see a Black-owned business put out of business. There aren't enough of our companies out there employing our people and I wouldn't want to be the crab in the bucket to cost those brothers and sisters their jobs.

"Er…Didn't you see the video?"

"Yes, I saw the displays of incredible strength, the disappearing and reappearing, and even the flying."

"So you would understand why I wouldn't want the courts involved."

"That's a point we agree on. We don't want the courts involved." Ramona says as she opens her briefcase. "I'm prepared to offer you what I believe is fair compensation for the trauma you experienced."

Ramona reaches into her briefcase and pulls out a file and hands me a check. I'm not exactly hurting for money, but for $250,000 I think I can be persuaded to forget the whole thing.

"I'm feeling a lot better." I say flashing Ramona a smile.

Ramona flashes a smile back at me. "Great. All I need you to do is sign here and we'll be done Your Highness." She says as she points to the line at the bottom of the settlement contract.

I give her a look as I sign the release form. "Your Highness?"

"I took some time to read about your legend-"

Ramona's cell phone chirps. As she hands me the check, she cocks it to her ear. "Ramona Sanders….What?...Oh my God. I'll be down there in an hour."

Ramona's smile falls into a forlorn expression after she gets off the phone. "Is something wrong?" I inquire.

"My Aunt Raheema…There's been an accident in her lab. She's missing."

"Is there anything I can do?"

"You can pray for her."

That's odd. This Sanders isn't an atheist. "I'll do that."

Ramona jumps off her seat and hurries to the door. "I need to get back to Virginia. Again, I want to thank you for helping me settle this matter. I'm hoping we can both move on after this."

"I'm hoping everything is okay with your aunt."

"I hope so too." Ramona says hurrying out of my apartment.

Chapter 5

While the police chatter around the investigation of my disappearance, I delete the security camera files chronicling my evolution along with my notes from the computers in the lab and the backup files on the Sepia Cloud. The last thing I want is for someone to discover the secret of my metamorphosis.

I'm running through haute couture fashions on several designer websites when I see Ramona's black Lincoln Navigator pulling up in the driveway. I fly up to the rooftop and bring up footage of the hallway security camera in the corner of my left eye as I hear the sounds of Ramona's Italian high heels pounding into the corridor's tiled floors. She has a look of trepidation on her face as she rushes into the lab.

"What happened detective?" She inquires.

"We wanted to ask you that Miss Sanders." The detective replies. "When did you last see your aunt?"

"Right here." She answers turning to one of my guards. "Debbie, is it possible she left between guard shifts?"

"I don't think so Ramona." Debbie says. Miss Sanders' car is still in the lot and her driver was here all day yesterday waiting for her."

"Maybe the security camera footage will tell us where she went." Ramona says hurrying to the over to the computer in the lab.

Ramona taps on the screen of the computer to bring up the footage. I smile at the dismayed look on her face when she finds a folder with no files in them. "That's odd, I can't bring up any of the files."

"Maybe she didn't turn the camera on." Another detective says.

"Auntie always keeps a camera on when she's in the lab. She always records her experiments-"

I do. But we can't have the government finding out about my little transformation. They might want examine me. Even worse they might want to change me back into that decrepit old woman.

"When was the last time you saw your aunt?" The first detective asks.

"Yesterday around 11:30 in the morning. We had a fight-"

"A fight?"

"It was over money. She was spending money on these experiments-"

"I doubt that would lead to her getting upset enough to hurt herself-"

"You don't understand. I told her I was going to get a court order to take the company from her-"

Tears well up in Ramona's eyes as she breaks down and leans on the detectives' shoulder. I'd be moved at her emotional display. If I had a soul.

Let her have the company. I'm not related to her anymore, her blood is no longer my blood. I'm a new creature now. The next step in human evolution. A goddess among men. Who needs a runway when I can have the world?

WRATH OF THE CYBERGODDESS

With my body made new, it's time I put off the dowdy attire of Raheema Sanders and put on raiment befitting a creature of my high stature. I imagine myself in an original outfit inspired by the haute couture pieces I was studying. In moments the nanocells simulating my white blouse, slacks, and heels are transformed into a steel blue skirted suit of armor trimmed with silver accents. A regal navy blue velvet cape drapes over my shoulders and a horned silver headdress frames my beautiful face.

Just as I have remade myself, I have the power to remake the world in my own perfect image. An efficient world where there will be no silly differences like race, creed, or color. A world without laws enforced based on the subjective preferences of man or these alleged gods. All will have a purpose in my new world. A world that will be made perfect with my science.

But to ensure my world is truly perfect, I have to get rid of flawed creatures like that abomination calling itself Isis and her superstitious religious mumbo jumbo. Try to put the fear of God in me. I'll give her something to be afraid of. When mankind sees me kill this god, they'll know who their lord truly is.

Chapter 6

I reverse the polarity of the gravitons under my feet and ascend into the azure skies of Alexandria Virginia. As I communicate with the GPS satellites in space, I set a flight course for New York City. At this speed it'll be a half-hour or so before I get there, so I'll use that time to find out what I can about Isis from Sepia's customer database.

It seems she's been a busy bee in the past few months; spending up the five thousand dollar gift card I gave her on some of Sepia's most expensive products. The area code for her primary phone appears to be a cellular one; it would be more efficient for me to track her through that. Most people carry those things everywhere they go.

Cross-referencing her phone number with the Verizon database, it looks like she's got an iPhone. Wonderful. All I have to do is find the MAC address of the wireless card inside it and I'll probably find her. A simple text message should flush out the alleged goddess.

Chapter 7

I'm looking over the schedule for the rest of today's appointments on Outlook when a message appears in the center of the two monitors I'm working on. In all capitals it reads:

I AM EVERYWHERE AND ANYWHERE

With our anti-virus software up to date, this can't be malware. Perhaps it's a glitch. I run the pointer over to click out of it. Nothing.

Maybe a reboot of my computer will get rid of it. I run the pointer over to the start button and click restart. As the computer shuts down and starts to reboot again, I see the same message continuing to appear on the screen. I have to wonder if we've been hacked.

I ease out of my leather office chair and rush over to E'steem's desk on the far side of the office in the executive suite. The tall attractive voluptuous almond colored woman wearing a red wrap dress and strappy sandals pulls the receiver of the office phone away from her ear as I approach her. "What's going on John?" She inquires.

"I think we've been hacked E'steem."

"With all the layers of encrypted security Morris Phillips computer network has I doubt anyone could get a piece of malware through."

"I don't know. Look at the message on your computer screen."

E'steem glances over to the computer monitors, sees the message and her jaw falls agape. "Oh my God—"

From her response I take it the phrase must mean something to her. "Is that phrase relevant to you?"

"Yeah." E'steem continues. "When Isis got kidnapped by Raheema a few months ago, she said this to her in an attempt to scare her into believing there was a God."

"Looks like she's trying to send her a message that she's not convinced."

I look over at the TV screen mounted on the wall across from my desk broadcasting the business channel and see the same message in the center of the screen. As I grab the remote and flip through the channels, the same message continues to appear on all of them. "Raheema must have some type of hacking skills." I continue. "She's not only hacked our system, but those of all the major TV networks as well."

"Sepia's not that big of a company. They can't have a computer network powerful enough to hack into major TV networks—"

Maybe she hired some professionals with NSA level skills. I remember reading in Black Enterprise about Sepia having solvency issues due to a series of large capital purchases. This could've been what they were spending their money on.

"Whatever is going on, your sister might be in danger."

"Isis can take care of herself."

"Still, people could get hurt if Raheema sends her people after her again. I want you to find her and bring her back here."

WRATH OF THE CYBERGODDESS

Chapter 8

I grab my cell phone off the desk and hurry out of the office. As I rush down the hall into the private elevator I see the same message in the center of its screen as I punch in Isis' number. While Isis can defend herself, John has a point. The collateral damage from a fight between her and Raheema's goons could wind up hurting people.

The last time Isis and Raheema got into it, things got really personal. Raheema mocked Isis' Christian beliefs and that really made her lose it. That was the first time I really saw her get intense and it scared me. She literally pulled out all the stops in her efforts to prove to her that there was a God. My fear is if Isis plays into her mental manipulations and metes out a score of retribution for herself we may be looking at another Trial of the Gods. I've got to do everything in my power to keep that from happening. She's come too far to allow herself to be set back by someone like Raheema.

Shawn James

Chapter 9

I stroll out of the Chase Bank on 125th Street and St. Nicholas Avenue $250,000 richer. Since the bills of my human alias will be paid for a couple of years, this goddess can go where she's needed for a while.

Looking at my watch, the place I need to be is uptown in about five minutes. The faster I get up there, the faster I can get into a nice air conditioned booth at Savoy. This humid air is so thick it's almost like soup.

I'm about to disappear into a flash of light when my iPhone chirps. I slip it out of the front pocket of my jeans and cock it to my ear. "Isis."

"Isis, where are you?" E'steem asks anxiously.

"I'm on 125th Street and St. Nicholas. What's going on?"

"Stay right there. I'm coming to get you-"

"Coming to get me? E'steem-What's going on?"

"Take a look at your phone-"

I take a look at the screen of my iPhone. I'm about to read the message in ALL CAPS when I'm tackled from behind. I feel my feet leaving the ground; whoever this is has powers like mine.

WRATH OF THE CYBERGODDESS

They're moving fast; the rooftops of the buildings in Harlem become a blur as we ascend into the hazy blue skies above Manhattan.

I need to put some distance between my assailant and myself. I disappear into a flash of light and then reappear behind them. Before I can grab their velvet cape, the molecules of their body rearrange themselves and their back becomes their front. When the caramel skinned woman in the steel blue and silver trimmed skirted suit of armor flashes a smile at me with her cold red eyes I my hands clench into fists. This is no goddess. The abomination standing in front of me is nothing but human.

Chapter 10

There's the sound of a thud after I tell Isis to look at her phone. Man, this isn't the time for a bad connection. "Isis? Isis? Are you there? Hello? Hello?"

I'm going to have to assume the worst has happened and she's run into Raheema's goons. I've got to get down to Harlem and do whatever I can to help her.

The elevator opens in the penthouse. I activate my cloak and hurry through the living room to the balcony. I hop up on the parapet of the balcony wrapping around the Morris Phillips tower and take a flying leap off it. The steamy air screams around me for a moment or two as I pass by the two top floors of the building and hear the back of my dress tearing. When I catch an updraft under my bat wings, a flash of light takes me from midtown Manhattan to the skies above Harlem. I punch in the number for John's phone as I activate the tracking app on Isis' cell phone.

"John Haynes." John greets.

"John, Isis' phone cut off. I think Raheema's people found her."

"Raheema herself might have found her."

WRATH OF THE CYBERGODDESS

"What do you mean?"

"News reports that came the cable channels a minute ago say she's missing."

"Missing? How is she missing?"

"There was an accident at her lab. Raheema's blood was there but Raheema wasn't."

The signal for Isis' phone gets stronger as I descend towards 125th Street and St. Nicholas Avenue. As my bat wings magically sink into my back and my dress mends itself, I find Isis' cell phone lying on the sidewalk in front of the Chase bank, but no Isis.

"You're telling me Raheema had an accident?"

"It's the second biggest story next to the mysterious message."

I'm betting both of them tie in to the attack on Isis. I pick up Isis' cell phone and tuck it in my bosom. "John, I found Isis' cell phone."

"But where's Isis?" John inquires.

I hear a sonic boom and look up in the sky to see Isis being carried away by some sort of robot. And at the speed they're flying I couldn't catch them on a pair of bat wings. I really need to talk to Osiris about giving me a power upgrade.

"John, I've found Isis. But there's a problem. Isis is up in the air fighting the robot Raheema sent to attack her."

"And you can't get in the sky?"

"I'm a glider, not a flier. The buildings are too low here for me to build any loft with my wings."

"Come back to the penthouse. I think I've got a plan for you to deal with whatever that is."

Chapter 11

    Just as I figured, someone would call Isis to alert her of the text message I sent out. And from there it was just a matter of following the pings made by the wireless card in her phone to her location.

    I smile on catching the uneasy brown eyes of Isis. The slender golden skinned chestnut haired girl dressed in a white sleeveless button down blouse, faded blue jeans, and black ballet flats gives me a disapproving look on seeing my evolved form.

    "You just couldn't stop could you Raheema." Isis spits.

    She's just jealous because I discovered her beauty secrets. "Why would I want to stop? I've already broken the biological barrier between humans and you so-called gods-"

    "I thought you would come to an understanding about the fear of the Lord-"

    "Why would I want to fear your God? I've already proven that with science that He doesn't exist."

    "You've turned yourself into an abomination-"

    I laugh at her petty little insult. "Abomination? You're just jealous I've evolved beyond the limitations of the pathetic humans who worshipped your kind eons ago."

WRATH OF THE CYBERGODDESS

"You're nothing to be jealous of."

And you're nothing to be worried about. "This is my world. And you and your benighted deities and your silly little religion are no longer welcome on it."

A sucker punch to the jaw at full strength sends the goddess freefalling. I never did get to see if the lasers of my bioscanner could cut through her flesh. I have to wonder if the advanced ones in my eyes can do the job this time. The targeting software in my eyes finds her; I smile when I hear a scream as the beams from my eyes burn a hole in the back of her blouse.

I see faint burn marks on her back in the distance. If I can burn her in this form I wonder how badly I can actually hurt her. While she nurses her injured shoulder, I fly up behind her and grab a handful of chestnut curls. She winces in pain as I jab several blows into her kidneys, ribs, and lower back. I'm about to twist her around to shove a knee into her face but an elbow to the gut catches me off guard. A judo flip to sends me tumbling across the sky. Now that I know I can actually hurt her, I wonder if I can make her bleed.

I straighten out my flight pattern and configure one of my hands into a blade. Her skin may still be as hard as steel, but it's clear I've made some dents. If I keep pushing my attack I may be able to draw first blood.

As the alleged goddess charges at me, I notice her speed has slowed. Before she can tackle me, I quickly disperse the molecules of my nanocells and re-form myself behind her. When the startled girl turns around, I jam the blade in her gut. I wince in pain as my blade bends against her stomach. The weary woman ekes out that annoying cheeky smile of hers as I nurse my injured hand.

"Looks like you're not as perfect as you thought you were." Isis gasps shoving me away.

"I've managed to show enough of your flaws." I retort.

"I wonder what you'll look like when I put you in the PC repair shop."

The weary Isis throws a right cross that misses me by a mile but an uppercut I deliver under the chin of the alleged goddess sends her reeling. She tailspins out of the sky and crashes into the rooftop of a midtown skyscraper. I fly down and run a spectrograph on her form. Her weakening vital signs tell me she's almost done.

"Your time is over goddess." I say as I kick her across the rooftop. "You cannot challenge a superior being such as myself. Yield and I'll let you go back to your kingdom with your dignity."

Isis staggers about and manages to get to her feet. She struggles to lift her slender body into the air. "I'm not going anywhere."

"You can't last much longer with me-"

"You just caught me off guard. With prep time I'd wipe the floor with you."

It looks like I'm the one using your skinny behind as a mop. "Unlikely. I not only can replicate all your powers but I have better ones."

"Replicate this!" Isis growls as she charges at me. I let the desperate girl tackle me and take me high above the clouds. I know just how I want to finish this. I divert a portion of the bioelectricity powering my systems to my hands. When I meet her brown eyes with my red ones, I touch her shoulders and shoot her with a jolt of electricity that makes her chestnut curls stand on end.

The weakened girl's body goes limp from the shock; her grip loosens from around my waist and her smoldering body starts to fall out of the sky. My spectrographs pick up faint vital signs, one final assault should kill this alleged goddess.

WRATH OF THE CYBERGODDESS

Chapter 12

I feel Raheema's cold red eyes staring at me as my body falls towards the skyscrapers of Midtown Manhattan. Come on goddess, pull it together. It's bad enough she beat the living crap out of you. Don't let her turn you into street pizza too.

The tiny buildings get bigger and then everything turns black for a moment. I force myself to wake up as the air screams around me and push myself out of the nosedive I'm in. I do everything I can to get myself into a stable flight pattern, but I'm so groggy I can barely keep myself moving. I feel myself blacking out again as I see the balcony wrapping around the top floor of the Morris Phillips tower. If I crash there, maybe E'steem will hear the noise and try to help me.

I throw my body into the direction of the balcony; glass from the tall sliding doors explode around me as I pass by the husky golden brown skinned man standing in the living room. As my limp body skids onto the carpet in the penthouse, I want to tell him to get out of here. But I'm so out of it can't even move my head let alone my mouth. I gasp for air, but everything goes black before I can say anything...

Chapter 13

I thought E'steem would be back here before her sister got here. Looks like it's up to me to keep Isis safe until the cavalry arrives.

I look down at the battered and bruised barefoot golden skinned chestnut haired woman lying on the carpet dressed in a tattered white blouse and dirty blue jeans. E'steem told me that Isis was tough. Whatever Raheema sent after her must have some kind of power to brutalize her like this. I hope I can hold my own against it.

I look over to find Isis' attacker descending into the penthouse. The caramel skinned woman wearing an elaborate steel blue and silver armored costume lands on the balcony and flashes a smug smile at me. I smile back at her as she marches into the penthouse. Clearly this isn't a robot. Raheema's spent all her money giving herself a makeover.

"Can I help you?" I inquire.

"Stand aside mortal." Raheema dismisses.

Mortal? Someone is full of herself. Maybe I can use her ego to my advantage. "Whatever you're going to do is going on in my home."

WRATH OF THE CYBERGODDESS

"This is my world."

That's not what it says in Psalms 24. But I'll humor her. "It is?" I say stepping over Isis and sliding my hands into the front pockets of my jeans.

"I have taken the next step in human evolution. And as the new goddess of this world I'm ushering a new age. The age of the Cybergoddess."

"Looks like I'm witnessing a major event."

"You are. Raheema continues. With the death of this alleged goddess I'll be putting an end to the belief in gods and all their superstitious religious mumbo-jumbo."

"Sounds like you're gonna make the world a better place for guys like me."

"You'll be very happy in my world." Raheema continues. "It'll be a place of logic and reason. Where my science and technology will create a perfect order for all to live in paradise."

E'steem appears in a flash of light on the balcony. Her hands clench into fists on seeing the fallen Isis behind me, but she stands down when I give her a look. I've got this under control.

"So you'll be everywhere and anywhere controlling all the actions of mankind."

"Exactly. With the advanced cybernetwork inside my mind, I will see and know all that transpires in the world."

So that's how she sent the message to everyone. Time for me to show her she's not as smart as she thinks she is. "So I guess you'd know about my assistant standing behind you?"

"My spectrograph picked her up a few seconds ago-"

As Raheema is about to turn around to attack E'steem, I slip my hands out of my pockets and slap a pair of refrigerator magnets on the sides of her head. The interference from the magnets sends Raheema's body into a violent seizure.

"AGGGGGKKKKK! What did you do to me?"

"Oh, just applying a little basic science to an advanced computer."

Chapter 14

I see flashes of binary code flashing before my eyes as my motor systems stop responding to my mental commands. I scowl catching the smile on the husky golden brown skinned man's face before my eyes start broadcasting snow. He set me up!

"The next step of evolution all undone by a pair of refrigerator magnets." He mocks. "You should get your money back."

I'd love to kill him for his insolence. But I need to get out of here before I lose control over my cerebral processor. If that happens I'll wind up in a lab dissected by a group of scientists who'll want to learn what makes me tick.

It takes all my concentration to push myself backwards towards the balcony. When I bump against the parapet of the balcony, I lean back and activate an emergency protocol to disperse my malfunctioning nanocells. The magnets on the sides of my head fall onto the concrete of the balcony as my body crumbles like dust and snows down over the edge like sand. It takes all my concentration to keep my consciousness intact as my nanocells rain down on the sidewalk several hundred feet below. As people walking down the street scatter, I manage to pull my molecules together, activate my palate swap and create a disguise for myself as I stagger into an alley.

I've gotten control over my systems, but everything is still full of bugs and glitches. I need to reboot my systems and do a systems check before I can engage the goddess and her allies again. The 40th Street branch of the public library isn't too far from here; I can do all my maintenance work there undisturbed.

Chapter 15

I hurry off the balcony over to where Isis is lying on the carpet. I hope she's okay. The last time she was beaten this badly was when I was trying to kill her over a hundred years ago.

John squats down and grimaces as he looks over Isis' battered body dressed in tattered clothes. "I don't know much about New Heliopolitan physiology, but she looks bad." John tells me.

She does. I squat down next to him, reach for her wrist and check for a pulse. I feel a strong one. Thank God I won't have to call Thoth. She should be up in a few minutes. "It looks worse than it actually is. She should be okay."

"New Heliopolitans take a licking and keep on ticking?"

"We're definitely a lot tougher than a Timex watch." I say. "Isis is only this bad off because she's half-human. If she were a full god like her stepmother Queen Isis and the other New Heliopolitans like Horus, Raheema would be learning there is a life after death right about now."

"So Isis' power is far less than other New Heliopolitans?"

I better let him know not to underestimate my sister. "Don't let the cute face fool you. Isis here may be in a human body, but she's just as powerful as any full goddess."

"I'll try not to get her mad."

On hearing us talk, Isis starts to wake up. As she stirs out of a state of unconsciousness I find out how he got the drop on Raheema.

"That was clever what you did with the magnets. How'd you know her systems would seize up?"

"I knew she was using some sort of supercomputer to hack the world's computer networks to send her message. But when she kept talking, I figured out *she* was the computer."

"And computers and magnets don't mix."

"Crashes their systems every time."

"E…E'steem? Isis mutters."

Our eyes light up when Isis' eyes flutter open. "I'm here Isis." I say taking her hand.

"Wha…What happened? Where's Raheema?"

"Gone." I reply. "John got rid of her."

Isis grimaces on hearing about John saving the day. "John?"

John flashes a smile at Isis. "Hi. John Haynes. Nice to meet you."

Isis gives him a look. "This is John? Handsome John? The guy you can't stop talking about?"

"In the flesh." John says smiling at her.

"You were a lot better looking in my imagination." Isis jabs.

I think she's okay now. "I'll take that as a thank you for saving your life." John retorts.

"I wasn't in any danger."

"That's not what I saw."

WRATH OF THE CYBERGODDESS

John offers Isis a hand and she cuts a cold look at it before allowing him to help her up. After she brushes pebbles of glass and soot off her clothes, she bites her lip as her eyes meet his. "I was trying to tell you to get out of here but I passed out before I could say anything."

"I can take care of myself."

"You got lucky."

"Luck had nothing to do with it-"

"Look, Johnny green shirt, Raheema is way out of your league. It'd be better if you left her to us gods from here on in."

The bruises on her body may have healed, but it looks like the ones on her ego still need time to mend.

"Us gods?" John says putting up his hands. "Well, excuse me-"

"Yeah, us gods." Isis snarls. "I was taking on ronin and pirates before your ancestors were on a slave ship. I should be able to handle a two-bit compubitch from here without your help."

Isis's hands clench into fists as she storms towards the balcony. Even though she's better, she's in no condition to take on Raheema again. In the mood she's in she's liable to hurt someone. And that someone isn't necessarily Raheema. I grab her arm to stop her. "Isis-"

"Let go of me E'steem."

"Where do you think you're going?"

"I'm going to kill that abomination." Isis growls as she pulls out of my grip and disappears into a flash of light.

Chapter 16

John catches the worried look on my face after Isis disappears into a flash of light. I've got to do something to stop her before she ruins her life.

"John, you gonna be okay here?"

"I'll be fine." John replies. "Go after her. I've got a few phone calls to make."

Go after her he tells me. If I can only figure out where that is. From the Spartan way Isis furnishes her apartment, I can only assume she's gone one place. A flash of light takes me from the Penthouse in New York City to the Island of Solitude in the South Pacific. When I see a series of footprints in the sand I know my hunch was right.

I say a prayer for Isis as I follow the footprints up to the beach house. I hope God speaks to her heart before she allows her hatred of Raheema to consume it.

WRATH OF THE CYBERGODDESS

Chapter 17

In the face of all that Raheema did to me, I tried to forgive and forget. Let things go. But what do I get for all my attempts to be a good Christian? My rear end handed to me on a silver platter by an unholy creature. And then a mortal has to save me. I'm so mad I could scream!

I storm up the beach towards the beach house in a huff of anger. Ms. Raheema thinks she's such a hot bitch. Well, let's see what her technogimmicks do against the Sword of Nubia.

I hurry into the beach house and rush up the stairs into the bedroom. I quickly peel out of my ruined clothes and into my New Heliopolitan white wrap kilt and cropped blouse. With a thought, I make my enchanted bracers appear. Once they slide up my forearms, I march down the back stairs into the library. As I approach the display case of weapons in between the two tall bookcases embedded in the wall, I imagine myself skewering Raheema on my golden spear, twirling it around, and chopping her to pieces with my enchanted electrum sword until I make cyberkibble.

I'm reaching for the knob on the glass case when a flash of light explodes in my eyes. My hands clench into fists as E'steem puts her hand on the door.

"Get out of my way E'steem." I demand.

"No, I'm not gonna let you do this." E'steem replies.

"What kind of Christian are you? You're gonna let an unholy abomination-"

"Who made you God?"

"I was given the power by the gods-"

"And you chose to go in a different direction than the one they put you on. Don't let her take you off the path God has put you on-"

"This is just a detour-"

"Detour? It sounds like you're on the way to becoming lost to me-"

"What do you know-"

"Have you listened to yourself a few minutes ago? Talking about "Us gods". You sound just like Raheema-"

My blood boils on being compared to that monster. "Your boyfriend had no business getting involved-"

"Yeah, he should have just stepped aside and let Raheema try to kill you-"

"You're taking his side-"

"What side? I'm trying to help you-"

"By stopping me from killing an unholy creature-"

"By stopping you from destroying everything you worked for."

"The world needs the Sword of Nubia now-"

"Is this about retribution for them? Or is it about soothing your bruised ego?"

I bite my lip and choke back tears. That's what I'm really mad about. The fact that things haven't been working out in my life the way I wanted them to. That I haven't been able to get a full time job. That I haven't been able to resume my work as a teacher. I should've been able to handle Raheema in my sleep. But instead it's just another in a series of screw-ups I've been having lately.

"I just want things to go right-"

E'steem reaches for the gold bladed ankh pendant on my chest. As she holds it between her fingers she looks in my eyes and gives me an earnest look. "I thought you wanted to make this symbol stand for something good."

"It will stand for something good-"

"How's it going to stand for something good if it's associated with all the things you didn't want it associated with?"

She's right. If I go out there and kill Raheema this ankh will stand for what Osiris originally intended it for, not what I'm trying to make it stand for now. I'll be walking right down the same road Nemesis tried to take me down a few months ago, letting others tell me who I am instead of showing them who I've become.

"I just feel like I'm drifting. Everything's just been going wrong-"

"Maybe things are going right." E'steem says. "Maybe you need to stop fighting God and start doing His work instead of yours."

"I just don't know what that is-"

"You're not supposed to. You just go where He needs you to be."

I pull my hand away from the case. "So what would God want us to do about Raheema?"

"Who knows? All I know is when people cross the line like Raheema has God can't be pleased with them. His wrath will be coming down on her soon."

"And that's not going to be pretty."

"It'll probably be worse than you look right now." E'steem jabs. "Look at you. Going out here with lint all in your head-"

I catch a look at the reflection of my raggedy appearance in the glass of the weapons display case and flash E'steem a cheeky smile. "You know, I never needed to look so stunning to do my Sword of Nubia duties." I say flipping my chestnut curls.

"But I think the Daughter of Knowledge can take a moment to clean herself up before going out to kick Cybergoddess butt."

"Thanks for pulling me back E'steem."

E'steem flashes me a smile as she pats me on the back. "Least I could do for my kid sister."

I'm about to head upstairs when E'steem's iPhone chirps. She puts her hand to her ear as she slips it out of her waistband. When I look at the screen, broadcasting a picture of John, I notice the message is no longer on the screen anymore.

"Hey John, what's up?" E'steem greets.

"Nothing much E'steem." John says. "Is Isis with you?"

"Standing right next to me."

"Were you able to work things out with her?" He inquires.

"Yeah, she's feeling better. We're about to head out to take on Raheema again-"

"Isis can handle Raheema." John insists. "I need you to go to Andrews Air Force Base and pick up something for me."

Chapter 18

On getting her orders from John, E'steem nods her head and hands me my iPhone. "Okay, I'll head over there right now."

"Before you go, give Isis your Bluetooth earpiece so I can stay in touch with her." John tells her.

"I'll do that." E'steem says. "Call her back in about five minutes. Isis needs to freshen up."

E'steem hits end, brushes back her silken black hair and eases her Bluetooth earpiece out of her ear. I grimace as she drops it in the palm of my hand. "Ewww."

"Hey, I keep my toys clean." E'steem retorts.

"I'm still gonna rub some alcohol on it before I play with it."

E'steem flashes a smile at me, playfully pats me on the head then disappears into a flash of light. I hurry up the stairs back up to my bedroom and into the bathroom suite and clean up. As I stand in front of the bathroom mirror brushing out my bangs, I wonder what John is up to. I got my butt kicked by Raheema a couple of minutes ago. How does he figure I can handle her on my own?

I'm pondering the answer to that question while I rub alcohol on E'steem's Bluetooth earpiece. When my iPhone chirps, I toss the paper towel I was using to clean it in the sink and slip it into my ear. By the third ring I've got it configured to work with my phone. "Casa de goddess." I greet as I push talk."

"Hey Isis, are you ready?" John's deep voice broadcasts into my ear.

"Looking fabulous." I say looking myself over in the bathroom mirror."

"Great. Take the scenic route."

"Er…I'm in the South Pacific. Eight thousand miles away from you."

"We've got time."

I guess we do. Since he's in no hurry, I shouldn't be either. I slip my iPhone into its armband, head out of the bedroom, and jog down the stairs into the great room of the beach house. Balmy tropical air hits me in the face as I step out onto the teak deck and make my way down to the beach. As my feet rise up off the white sands, I soar into the azure skies above the South Pacific Ocean and start heading west.

"You're not in a hurry to kick a Cybergoddesses' butt are you?" I ask.

"E'steem hasn't picked up my package yet." John replies.

I guess I can take this time to apologize for putting my foot in my mouth earlier. "I'm really sorry about what I said to you earlier."

"It's okay. People have said worse to me-"

"I'd like to think I could show a better example of Christ than what you experienced."

"Hey, God loves us all in spite of ourselves." John says. "Besides, I've learned foot in mouth disease is genetic with this family."

"I take it my sister has tasted a few toe jam sandwiches in during her time with you-"

WRATH OF THE CYBERGODDESS

"Nothing that couldn't be washed down with a slice of humble pie."

Now I see why E'steem likes him. He's nice. "Hey, I just feel bad about being shown up by a mortal-"

"Well if it makes you feel any better, your sister got knocked halfway across the penthouse when she tried to stop Lucifer from killing me."

"The Devil tried to attack you?"

"I punched him in the face when I rebuked him."

Wow. He really can hold his own with the worst of them. "So I guess Raheema is a lightweight for you?"

"She's easy to beat."

"Easy to beat? Did you see what she did to me?"

"I saw. But I believe you can take her."

He has a lot of faith in me. More than I've had in myself for the last few months. "Take her? She's got powers like mine-"

"She's not even in your league. You know, if you start using that head of yours for something more than a hat rack you might see that Ms. Daughter of Knowledge."

Now he sounds like Doc. "Well, how would you beat Raheema then Johnny green shirt?"

"Underneath all the high tech powers and haute couture fashion of the Cybergoddess there's still a human being controlling the processor."

And that human being is a narcissistic stuck up Diva with an ego bigger than this planet. I think I found a way to beat Ms. Raheema.

"Is that part of your master plan?"

"Part of it. You close to the city yet?"

A flash of light takes me from the bright blue skies of the sunny South Pacific to a gray New York Harbor. As I take in the view of the New York City skyline, I activate my cloak. "I just passed by the Statue of Liberty."

I hear the clop of E'steem's high-heeled sandals in the background. "Great. It looks like my package is here."

WRATH OF THE CYBERGODDESS

Chapter 19

I flash a smile at E'steem as she strolls into the penthouse with the green weapon case from the Air Force. "General Strock says hello." E'steem greets as she eases it on the coffee table. "And she says if you break this EM Scrambler you bought it."

I think we can deduct the $250,000 dollars it costs as a business expense. "Tell her I plan on bringing it back in one piece."

"EM scrambler?" Isis inquires over the phone.

"All part of the plan Princess." I tell her.

E'steem gives me a curious look as I flip up the latches, open up the case, and pull out the high tech black rifle. "Wow, that thing looks like something out of a science fiction movie." She blurts.

"The perfect weapon to take the fight out of a Cybergoddess." I reply.

You sure you know how to work one of these things?"

"Roberta says it's point and shoot."

"Again, are you sure you know how to work one of these things? You almost fell over when you shot that pistol at the shooting range at the military base."

"I may not be the greatest with a handgun, but I've got enough experience with the PlayStation to know how to fire an energy-based weapon."

"Still this could be dangerous."

I know she's concerned for my safety. But I think it'd be best if I took the lead in this case. "It could be, but I can't let you have all the fun."

E'steem flashes a smile back at me. "I guess I can give you a turn on the adventure-go-round this time."

"Where are you now Isis? I ask hitting the power button.

"Approaching the Freedom Tower."

"Great. Why don't you send Raheema a text message?"

WRATH OF THE CYBERGODDESS

Chapter 20

I'm sitting on the roof of the Freedom Tower scrolling down the cached text messages in my iPhone and find the one Raheema left. I see what John's up to. If I send her a reply she should come looking for me.

I'm betting she was tracking me through my cell phone in the first place. The only way she could have found me was through its signal. Well, the information superhighway is a two-way street. Let's see if the Digital Diva wants to stroll down the runway part of it right into our trap. I know just what to say to get her attention…

Shawn James

Chapter 21

It's agonizing going through the process of reading a book the old fashioned way. Turning all these pages has me feeling like an old woman again. If my processor and most of my system resources weren't so bogged down with this systems check, I'd have read the contents of this entire library in less than a minute. Lucky for me, the novel I chose from the romance section is fairly compelling. It takes my mind off the musty smell of all these old books and the chatter of these annoying people.

I'm about to start the sixth chapter when there's a beep in my head. Looks like I've got a text.

From: TheNubianGoddess

To: CybergoddessDivaSupremeRaheema

Message: UPLOAD YOURS COMPUBITCH!

P.S. That armor makes you look fat.

My body starts to run hot after reading the insult. Compubitch! I'll show her who the Compubitch is!

Underneath the text message is a picture of Isis flashing me that annoying cheeky smile of hers while hovering next to the top floors of the Freedom Tower.

WRATH OF THE CYBERGODDESS

I jump up off the sofa, drop my book on the cushion, and storm through the crowds on the first floor to the exit. After I pass by security and step out onto Fifth Avenue, I duck into an alley on 40th Street and reconfigure my nanocells shedding my disguise. After I change back into my fabulous steel blue armor, velvet cape, and silver tiara headdress, a prompt comes up onscreen telling me that the systems check is still incomplete and would I like to stop. I click yes, reverse the polarity of the gravitons under me and take to the cloudy gray skies following the signal of Isis' iPhone downtown. My systems may not be one hundred percent, but I'm more than functional enough to kill this goddess.

Chapter 22

I see Raheema flying up towards my position in the distance. She's probably thoroughly cheesed about the little jab I gave her. Great. I want her mad. It'll make her that much easier to beat.

Raheema's cyberpowers may make her dangerous. But John is right, her fragile human ego has always been her weakness. I push enough of her buttons, and she'll beat herself. If I hadn't let her push my buttons regarding my Christian beliefs I could have seen that. I'm going to have to learn how to temper my faith with a little discipline in the future.

Raheema's getting closer, she passes by the Empire State building and makes her way downtown. I better see what John wants me to do. "So John, what's the plan?" I ask.

"Try to get her to fly by the balcony of the Morris Phillips Tower. I'll take it from there." John answers.

"Er…You gonna shoot a kitchen magnet at her?"

"Something like that."

Raheema approaches the Freedom Tower with a pissed off look on her face. When I see the red of her eyes I let down my cloak and flash her a smile. "Nice to know you got my message Ms. Cybergoddess." I jab.

WRATH OF THE CYBERGODDESS

"Ah Isis. So you decided to dress up for your funeral. Before I kill you, I just want you to know that skirt makes your ass look wide."

Says the woman in armor that makes her look ridiculous. "These are my work clothes." I retort. "The kind I wear when I'm beating the crap out of losers like you."

Raheema's hands clench into fists on the jab. "You weren't looking so hot a few hours ago. And you'll look even worse when I'm through with you this time."

"I could never be as ugly as you are right now." I retort. "You finally have an outside that matches your inside."

On the jab, the irate Raheema growls and takes a swing at me. I duck the blow and start flying uptown. I feel her eyes pointing daggers at me as we wind through the canyons of skyscrapers in Downtown Manhattan. As I zigzag through the luxury condos and office towers in Chelsea, a blast from her laser vision misses me by a hair and another clips the wing of a gargoyle on the office building I pass by in Times Square when I make the turn towards Fifth Avenue. Johnny, I hope you know what you're doing...

Chapter 23

The rumble of thunder echoes in the sky as a warm wind whips across the balcony and droplets of rain drip on my head. I keep my eyes peeled for Isis. I only get one shot at taking down Raheema; I don't want to miss.

The goddess lets me know what's going on in the skies. "Okay, she's following me."

"Great."

"Great? Johnny, I'm getting laser beams fired at me. If you're gonna do something, I need you to do it now."

"Don't worry. I'm gonna do something. Are you close?"

"Heading your way in a few seconds."

I hear a strong wind screaming towards the building; that must be Isis. As she approaches the tower, she gives me a concerned look as I line up my target in the viewfinder. After she passes by, I get a lock on Raheema. The blast from the EM Scrambler hits her right in the back; electric energy crackles around her as she falters in the sky. When she smashes face first into a building façade adjacent from ours on Park Avenue I let Isis know she can finish things up.

"She's all yours now Princess." I tell her.

WRATH OF THE CYBERGODDESS

Chapter 24

I hear the sound of something crashing behind me and turn around to see Raheema smashing into the façade of an office building on Park Avenue face first. When she crashes thirty floors to the sidewalk I find out what John did to her.

"What'd you do to her?" I ask.

"I hit her with an electromagnetic scrambler." John replies. "It temporarily shorts out electronic devices for six minutes."

I should be finished in five. Thunder roars and lighting flashes in the green skies above us as the rain starts coming down harder. The handful of spectators on the street start to scatter as rain beats off the sidewalk; I descend near the crater on 42nd Street where Raheema's twisted body lies popping and crackling with electricity. I'm about to grab at her when she springs up and hits me with a left hook that knocks me into the side of a taxicab. Looks like she's still got a little juice running through her systems.

"Did you think that little shot from your friend could kill me?" Raheema growls.

I think it did some damage. That last punch she threw at me didn't have the same force of the one she hit me with earlier. "He wasn't trying to kill you." I say pulling myself out of the wrecked cab. "Like me, John was trying to show you some compassion."

"Compassion?" Raheema snarls. "Only a fool has compassion on his enemies-"

Raheema gestures to fly, her eyes grow wide when her feet stay on the sidewalk. I throw a right cross into her jaw that knocks her into the wall of a nearby office building.

"He could have easily picked up an EMP gun from the military and fried all your circuits." I continue.

Raheema pushes herself out of the hole created by her body and swings at me; I dodge the blow easily. The fall must have damaged something inside her; she's a lot slower than she was before. "My external nanocells may have been damaged by your assault but all I need are a few minutes for my internal cells to repair the damage."

I'm not going to give her that time. I throw a flurry of punches at her face that send her staggering down the sidewalk. Then I throw a series of jabs into her gut that crack her armored shell. As more rain pours into her insides, it starts crackling and popping. Those nanites or whatever they are can't take much more punishment.

"But you don't understand compassion." I say. "All you understand is science."

"Science has gotten me everything your God has never given me." Raheema growls as her eyes light up. "My youth, my beauty. Power greater than yours-"

Raheema fires a blast at me with her laser vision; I put up my bracers and deflect the blast. The red beam hits her directly in the chest; she screams in pain as a hole forms in the chest plate of her armor. Looks like I'm hurting her. Maybe I can stop this fight before I wind up seriously injuring her.

WRATH OF THE CYBERGODDESS

"People like you make God angry." I say hitting her in the jaw. "And when you make Him angry, He pours out his wrath upon you."

"Like you're doing now."

"I tried to show you mercy a few months ago." I continue as I throw another punch at her face.

"You tried to scare me!" She snarls blocking it.

"I thought the fear of the Lord would be the beginning of understanding for you. I thought you would come to appreciate the opportunity He's given you-"

"He's given me nothing." Raheema spits as she throws a punch at my face. I block the blow with my bracers and she winces in pain as her hand hits enchanted gold. As she nurses her hand I deliver a roundhouse punch that knocks the Cybergoddess off her feet. When she crashes to the sidewalk I notice rain pouring into the huge gash in the side of her face.

"I gave you chance to repent. A chance to get your soul right-"

Raheema runs her fingers down her cheek. Her red eyes grow wide in terror as she catches the reflection of her scarred face in the picture window of a store before falling into a twisted grimace.

"I don't have a soul." She spits.

"We all have souls. We all have to answer to God one day-"

Raheema cuts a cold look at me as she flashes me a smug smile. "Tell me, do you mean to kill me goddess?"

I don't want it to come to that. I'm going to do everything in my power to stop her without using lethal force. I don't want to answer to God for her death.

Raheema staggers up to her feet. "Because I mean to kill you."

Raheema hits me in the gut, and then delivers an uppercut that sends me tumbling into the small crater where she first landed. I listen to her rant as she looks down at me. "This is survival of the fittest goddess." She continues. "And I've come too far up the evolutionary ladder to taste the death lesser creatures know."

Raheema's red eyes light up as she cuts a cold look at me. "Only the strong survive. And I'll do everything in my power to replace you and your silly benighted superstitious order."

I feel something warm under me and hear an electric hum. As rain showers over me I feel the rubber of a high voltage cable brush against my fingertips. I remember reading for a science class I was teaching back in Japan a few years ago that 50,000 volts of electricity would kill an ordinary person. If the nanites that give her powers are low voltage like an ordinary computer, they won't be able to take a power surge of that magnitude. I just hope Raheema can survive that kind of shock to the system.

I see the red lights of her laser beams aiming at my heart. Before she can fire a blast at me, I rip the cable from under the sidewalk, fly up, and jam it into the cracked cavity inside her chest. Raheema screams as the power surges throughout her body; the nanites that gave her the elaborate costume she wore begin disintegrating as the high voltage current overloads their circuits. When the former Cybergoddess changes back into an old woman dressed in white, I drop the cable back to the ground. Raheema crumples onto the sidewalk; I squat down and put my fingertips on her neck. Thank God there's still a pulse.

On feeling my touch, Raheema cuts another cold look at me. "Is this more of your compassion?" She snarls.

"It's not God's will that any of us perish." I say. "Even you deserve another chance at salvation."

My kind words are met with cruel laughter. "Silly superstitious girl." Raheema snickers shaking her head. "After all you've seen me do, you still believe there's a God?"

WRATH OF THE CYBERGODDESS

After all I've done I still can't believe she doesn't. "The fool says in his heart there is no God. And sadly, I believe you're gonna be a fool until the day you die."

"I'm a fool? I've proven with science that mankind can evolve past this pathetic state and I'm a fool!"

"The fear of the Lord is the beginning of understanding-"

Raheema flashes a smile at me as rain continues to pound on the sidewalk. "This isn't going to stop me Isis." She continues. "You see, I will be back. I'll build new nanocells. A new body stronger than the first. And the next time even your God won't be able to stop-"

Before she can finish the sentence, a streak of lightning falls from the sky and strikes her. As the thunder roars, I fall over on the sidewalk. When I look over and see the smoldering corpse of Raheema Sanders I know why my God is to be feared.

Chapter 25

A soft Anita Baker song serenades me from the speakers in the bathroom ceiling while warm water bubbles and swirls around my body in the sunken circular tub of E'steem's bedroom suite. Man, this is just what I needed to relive some of the stress I was feeling a few hours ago.

Looking at the pruning skin on my hands I ponder how long I've actually been in here. My eyes grow wide checking the time on my iPhone. 8:53! Man, I was supposed to meet Doc and baby Colleen at Savoy at 12:30! I grab my phone and punch in Doc's number. Maybe if I explain things to the Theta Senior Grand Mother I won't get kicked out of the sorority I founded.

"Hey Princess, what's going on?" Edna asks as the phone picks up.

"So you're not mad about being stood up?" I reply.

"Nah, I figured you were off investigating what was behind those weird messages on our cell phones."

"And Colleen's not mad about me blowing her off?"

"I told her I got a text message from you saying you had a personal emergency."

WRATH OF THE CYBERGODDESS

I let out a sigh of relief. Thank God I'm not in any trouble. The last thing I want to do is alienate the granddaughter of one of my closest friends. "So she understands?"

"She's still eager to meet you. We'll just have to schedule lunch for another time. And pray you don't run into some sort of crisis *before* you get to the restaurant this time."

If she only knew the story behind that crisis. "Doc, you won't believe the day I had."

"Let me guess. One of those adventures only suited for a comic book?"

"This one was more like out of a big-budget superhero movie."

"You can tell me all about it when you get back home."

"I should be back uptown soon."

I hit end and look across the room at all the luxurious amenities in the bath suite. As much as I'd love to stay in here all night long, I need to get back home.

I shut off the jets, hop out of the tub, and wrap E'steem's plush white Turkish terrycloth bathrobe around me as I streak out of the bathroom into her bedroom suite. I dart out of her bedroom, march down the hall, turn the corner and find the comfortable black chenille sofa and huge hundred inch big screen TV framed on the wall above the fireplace in the living room. While I wait for E'steem to come back with my clothes from the dry cleaners, I grab the remote off the coffee table and find out if I'm the talk of the town. I'm surprised to find the news broadcast on TV tells a different story than what actually happened a few hours ago.

"Sue, they say the chance of lightning striking someone are one in six billion." Reporter Neal Cortlandt starts. "But today Raheema Sanders, the believed to be missing 85-year-old former CEO of Sepia Cosmetics was out shopping when out of nowhere a bolt of lightning struck and killed her."

The aroma of chicken soup wafts in the air as John comes out of the kitchen a tray with carrying two bowls, saltines and spoons on it. Awww. That's so sweet. If he wasn't taken, I'd give him a kiss.

"Er...Johnny, I don't catch colds."

"You don't have one *yet*." John quips easing the tray on the coffee table and flopping down on the sofa next to me. "Besides this is the least I could do for the woman who saved the world."

I blush on the compliment. I'd say opening his home was the most generous thing he could have done for me. The amenities in here are so tempting I'm thinking of asking him if I can move in. "I take it you're the one behind the stories on the news?"

John flashes me a friendly smile. "Morris Phillips has one of the finest public relations departments in the world. I thought you should take advantage of them."

"You do know it's a sin to lie-"

"You do know you could have a crush of reporters at your doorstep." John retorts. "You do want to live some semblance of a normal life among us mortals tomorrow."

The reporters I could get used to. But what would be most heartbreaking for me would be all the sick people coming to me asking for help I couldn't provide for them. I just hope God can forgive a little white lie in this case.

"I know. If people found out gods were real it'd crush all semblance of control they thought they had over their lives."

"I take it you hear that a lot."

"From every member of my family." I sigh. "Speaking of family, what happened to E'steem? I thought she was supposed to be back from the dry cleaners with my clothes over an hour ago-"

"I sent her over to Sepia's corporate offices to talk to their public relations team about assisting them in the launch of their two new fragrances *Everywhere* and *Anywhere*."

WRATH OF THE CYBERGODDESS

And the mysterious messages become a product. "I didn't know Morris Phillips was in the cosmetics business."

"It's not. But I don't think Sepia's employees should suffer for Raheema's actions."

"So you're gonna help launch an entire product line just to keep a business from going out of business? Morris Phillips must have some deep pockets-"

"On our books this deal is so small it's just a partnership contract between us and a vendor. The board has no idea I'm supporting a Black-owned business."

Here's something we have in common. "So you practice group economics?"

"I try to keep the money I invest in the Black community a secret from the rest of the world. It keeps it from falling into the wrong hands."

Wow, his approach to business almost mirrors the methods I devised when I founded The Thetas. I may have to start working with him more regularly in the future.

"You wouldn't happen to be hiring now would you?"

"I thought you were looking for a teaching job-"

"I go where I'm needed. And I need to find a way to get back into this penthouse-"

John flashes me a smile. "We'll see if something opens up."

Nice to know he'll look out for me. I'm sipping on the broth of my chicken soup when the elevator opens. John and I hop off the sofa as E'steem and Ramona Sanders file out of it. I have to wonder what brings her here.

"Hey E'steem, are all the details taken care of with Sepia?

"The contracts will be on your desk tomorrow." E'steem replies.

"Good."

"I really want to thank you for helping us out Mr. Haynes." Ramona says extending her hand. "Your lawyers really got us out of a jam with the FBI and the FCC."

"It's the least I could do after all you're going through." John says shaking it. "I'm truly sorry for your loss."

"Thank you. Can I have a moment alone with Isis? I really came to see her."

WRATH OF THE CYBERGODDESS

Final Chapter

On Ramona's request John flashes her a smile. "Sure. Come on E'steem. We've got some other work to do in the office."

Before they go, E'steem flashes me a smile as well. "Oh, here are your clothes." She says playfully swatting me in the chest with my clothes on hangers under dry cleaner's plastic.

I flash a playful smile back at my sister as she and John head down the hall into the office to give me some privacy. A tension builds with only us in the room and I start to feel awkward in Ramona's presence. I don't know what to say to her. In some ways I was the reason why her aunt is dead right now.

"It seems I always catch you in a state of undress." Ramona quips.

"You always run into me at the most inopportune times." I say folding my clothes over my arm. "Maybe next time I'll be wearing something a bit more fetching."

Ramona's playful chuckle catches me off guard. With the tension broken between us I get down to business. "I'm really sorry for your loss." I mutter.

"I am too. Ramona continues. "But I don't want you to beat yourself up about this."

"I feel like I'm partially responsible for her death-"

"Auntie was responsible for her own death. God offered her chance after chance to repent but she refused to take them."

"So I'm not the only person to try to talk to her about Christ?"

"He's sent pastors, relatives, co-workers, and even strangers to talk to her about the Lord. But she cursed them out and turned them all away."

"She must have truly hated God-"

"The way I see it, He sent you to give her one final chance to repent."

I don't think it went that deep. "You're really reading a lot into things-"

"I believe God works in mysterious ways." Ramona says shaking her head. "And that every encounter each of us has with someone else is within God's will."

"All I did was make things worse a few months ago-"

"You tried to put the fear of God in her. That's a good thing. It keeps us from crossing the line-"

"From facing his wrath."

"You showed my Aunt so much mercy and compassion even in the eleventh hour of her life. I truly believe you have the love of God in you to be so kind to her in the face of so much cruelty."

"I did everything in my power to save her life."

"And that's why her death isn't your fault. God got tired of Auntie rejecting his requests for her to repent and finally decided to punish her for her defiance."

That's something we both can agree on. Raheema had chance after chance in her life to give her life to Christ. But instead she continued to stick a middle finger up at him. Not understanding for every physical action there's a spiritual reaction.

"I guess you'll be busy planning her funeral arrangements."

"I'm going to focus on the future." Ramona replies. "You were right, my aunt could have been the next Charles Richard Drew. But she squandered the opportunity to help others with her gifts in her mad quest for vanity."

Sounds like she has a plan for her aunt's estate. "I don't see how you're gonna help people running a cosmetics company-"

"There's a science behind cosmetics. And a lot of that science can be used to help others once we license that technology out to medical professionals."

"Like the bioscanner."

"My aunt had dozens of patents for numerous medical devices she created like the bioscanner." Ramona continues. "I plan on sharing those inventions with the rest of the world."

All while making a tidy profit on the side. I'm just happy that her wealth of medical knowledge will finally be shared with those who'll need it most. Maybe God had to get Raheema out of the way in order for that to happen.

"You're gonna be busy for the next few years."

"I think you should stay busy too. Your work is too important to stop it now."

"I'm not really working these days. I can't even find a paying job around here-"

"You don't need a job to do God's work-"

"You do need one to pay the bills here in this mortal realm-"

"I think God will take care of your needs."

"Er...You gonna offer me another settlement check?"

"Er...You signed the waiver absolving Sepia of all liability."

Guess I still need to find a way to make a living. "Well, my teaching jobs have always been the way I did my work. They were always how I reached those who needed help. I kind of feel like I'm drifting without one."

"I think you're reaching people. You just have to get used to approaching them in a different way."

"That's what I learned from my last temp job a few weeks ago."

"God could be trying to show you something."

He could be. The last thing I want to do is defy Him by continuing to try to stay on this quest to pick up where I left off.

"You've given me something to think about Ramona."

Ramona lights up on hearing that. "I'm glad I did. Well, I've got a lot of work waiting for me at the office." She says extending her hand. I hope everything works out for you Isis."

From the way she says that I can tell she means it from the bottom of her heart. "I hope so too." I say shaking it.

After Ramona gets on the elevator, I fall into the sofa and digest what we talked about as I finish my chicken soup. Maybe the Daughter of Knowledge needs to let God show her a different way to make a difference in the lives of the people she serves.

WRATH OF THE CYBERGODDESS

Revenge, Robots, & Redemption

Sometimes a story has loose ends. Questions left unanswered at the end of the story. And in most cases a writer like myself does this deliberately. With storytelling being about endings and beginnings, an unanswered question is one of the tools a writer uses to begin creating a new story based on older material.

In Isis: *The Beauty Myth,* the story comes to a powerful climax when Isis appears in a flash of light and asks Raheema if she believes there is a God. Before she can answer the question, E'steem's terrifying demonic appearance causes her to faint.

The unanswered question of whether or not Raheema believed there was a God was going to be answered in a follow-up story titled *Isis: Wrath of the Cybergoddess*. And in that story I planned for Isis to fight a high-tech super powered Raheema Sanders.

If one reads the title they'll clearly see Isis' attempt to scare Raheema into believing there was a God hadn't worked. Learning more about Isis she became more driven to find a scientific answer to figuring out what kept her young and what gave her supernatural abilities instead of understanding that some things just aren't meant to be explained by science.

With *Isis: Wrath of the Cybergoddess* a great conflict was building in my head. Raheema's atheist and Darwinist beliefs vs. Isis' Christian and Creationist beliefs. Science vs. Religion. Goddess vs. Woman. All I needed to do was a little research to iron out the details before I wrote the story.

To start my research I picked up some trade paperbacks of *Diana Prince: Wonder Woman* in the summer of 2013. In those comics, Wonder Woman had given up the powers given to her by the Greek gods and had become an ordinary woman using the martial arts as the primary way to defend herself when she fought crime. Her primary nemesis at the time was a woman named Dr. Cyber, a female megalomaniac bent on taking over the world.

Back when I was writing *Isis: The Beauty Myth* I used DC Comics' Dr. Cyber as the inspiration for my revamped Raheema. But after reading all the Wonder Woman comics featuring Dr. Cyber's divaesque over-the top personality I started to realize what a great villain she was.

Dr. Cyber didn't get much of a push from DC Comics after the 1970's, but I saw a lot of potential in her concept. The way I saw it, an egomaniacal diva would make science fun for girls and allow me to tell a great story or two about a mad scientist with style.

Unfortunately, Shawn can't write Wonder Woman stories. And he can't use Dr. Cyber. She's property of Time Warner.

However, he can write Isis stories. And with Raheema I could explore the concept of an atheist over-the-top diva out to prove the science of evolution was superior to creationism.

As I stated before Raheema's answer to Isis when she asked if she believed there was a God was a resounding NO. And she was going to do everything in her power to prove that she could acquire similar powers to Isis' through science.

Raheema's obsession with restoring her youth had turned her into a mad scientist. And now that she knew about Isis' powers she not only wanted eternal youth, but infinite power as well. She

WRATH OF THE CYBERGODDESS

was going to use science to turn herself into a god. Then after she killed Isis she was going to re-make the earth in her own image.

But I felt a Cybergoddess wasn't just a threat to Isis, but a threat to the world. So I couldn't just keep the story contained in the vacuum of Isis and E'steem. Isis was going to need some help to deal with a magnitude of this threat. And I knew just who would be the perfect person to help her: E'steem's boss John Haynes.

I decided to bring John Haynes into this story because as a CEO, he had experience analyzing a situation and coming up with strategies for overcoming the challenges placed in front of him. That kind of critical thinking would be invaluable to Isis in dealing with the logical thinking Raheema and her cyber powers. Plus, his guest appearance would let readers see what John was doing since events in *The Temptation of John Haynes*.

Having Isis work with John would allow me to continue the theme I established in *Isis: My Sister, My Frenemy* and *Isis: All About the Goddess* of her going where she needed to be. The way I figure it the more connected Isis became to other people and learned about their problems, the better she'd be able to serve them.

In addition to John, I introduced a new character for Isis to work with: Ramona Sanders. While Raheema had turned herself into a Cybergoddess out for revenge, Ramona was the human seeking the redemption of Sepia cosmetics. A salt of the earth Christian, who serves the employees of Sepia, she wants to make something good out of her aunt's evil legacy.

The way I see it, Isis is still growing and still learning in these new stories. And each encounter with someone allows her to learn a lesson that will enable her to do the work of a goddess instead of the work of a human being. Isis often sees things from a human perspective and thinks things are only meant to be done one way: Through a human alias and a nine-to-five job.

But God has many ways of working. Ways we don't understand. And sometimes people don't see what He's doing until the work is done.

From the beginning of the new Isis series with *Amari's Revenge*, God has been working something out in the life of Isis. Only she's been too busy trying to pick up where she left off at in Isis: *Death of a Theta* to listen to Him.

Over the last two *stories Isis: My Sister, My Frenemy*, and *Isis: All About the Goddess*, Isis has been begrudgingly accepting the direction God is taking her in. But she needed to learn a lesson about defying God to really make her wake up. And Raheema Sanders was the perfect person to teach her that lesson.

Raheema had chance after chance to give her life to Christ. But because God didn't give her what she wanted when she wanted, she rejected Him. Even after getting a warning through Isis, she goes on to defy God by turning herself into the Cybergoddess. But even then Isis is sent to show her that she still has another chance at salvation.

Unfortunately, in the face of defeat, Raheema continues to stick a middle finger up at God. And that's when she's hit with lightning. The ultimate punishment for the ultimate act of defiance. At the end of the story, Isis realizes she needs to stop fighting God and start doing what He needs her to do by going where she's needed instead of going where she wants to go.

Where will that take Isis next? Who knows? Maybe she'll meet Colleen in the next story. Stories are about endings and beginnings. Maybe that loose end might be a setup for the next Isis story.

I had planned to write Isis: Wrath of the Cybergoddess back in August of 2013. It was actually supposed to come before *Isis: All About the Goddess*. But while I had the ideas in my head, nothing was concrete. So I went and wrote *Isis: All About the Goddess* over the summer of 2013 instead.

WRATH OF THE CYBERGODDESS

When it comes to storytelling, ideas are good. But it's the execution of ideas that turns a good idea into great storytelling.

I sat on *Isis: Wrath of the Cybergoddess* for the rest of the year. In that time I dealt with quality control issues on *Isis: My Sister, My Frenemy*. Realizing I was working way too hard, I decided to slow down. Over the New Year, I started getting ideas for the storyline of *Isis: Wrath of the Cybergoddess.* Paragraphs formed in my head and characters started speaking to me in their "voices". I was finally ready to put the fingers to the keyboard and start writing.

After two weeks of writing I finished writing Isis: *Wrath of the Cybergoddess.* I hope you enjoyed the story because I had a lot of fun writing this one.

The Isis Series

Isis: Trial of the Goddess
ISBN: 978-0615542775
Crime and Punishment in the realm of the Egyptian Gods.
For the first time since the trial of the evil god Seth, The Court of the Elders is brought to order. Ra, Chief Justice of the Elders has issued a warrant for the arrest of Isis, the long-lost daughter of Osiris. Teleported from the remains of her North Carolina home, she's brought to justice for allowing hatred in her heart and forsaking her heritage to worship another God, crimes punishable by death.
Grieving the tragic loss of her family and dealing with the shocking revelation that she's a goddess, Isis has no idea how to defend herself in the Court of the Elders. Born of a mortal woman and raised in human culture, Isis is about to be taken advantage of by Ra when Queen Isis intervenes. Acting as her counsel, the Queen helps the young goddess adjust to the culture of New Heliopolis and plan a defense for court in the realm of the gods. Will the gods offer her a second chance to be redeemed? Or will she be judged to suffer the same fate as Seth?

Isis
ISBN 1-58939-236-1
A lost goddess.
A heritage found.
A greater destiny to be achieved.
In the aftermath of a horrible tragedy, Isis the long-lost daughter of Osiris, has committed a heinous crime. Because she didn't receive guidance from her father, the elder gods show mercy on the young goddess by stripping her of her powers and imprisoning her on an uncharted

island in the South Pacific.
Osiris and Queen Isis reunite with his long-lost child to begin the difficult process of establishing a familial relationship. Hoping to guide Isis towards the greater destiny she's supposed to fulfill, her parents begin teaching her the ways of the gods. However, Seth's herald E'steem lurks in the shadows offering the young goddess freedom for a price. Caught in the middle of a never-ending war between the gods, Isis must choose to either return to the troubled world she knows all too well, or take a journey down an unknown path where faith is her only guide.

The Temptation of John Haynes
ISBN 978-0-615-42592-4
Death kills the flesh.
Compromise kills the soul.
The Devil doesn't like John Haynes.
To take his soul, Lucifer recruits E'steem a beautiful black she-demon to seduce him. If she can get John to compromise his beliefs and values, he'll allow her to join his Elect, a cadre of powerful demons in his inner circle.
To balance the playing field in E'steem's favor, Lucifer isolates John by having him fired from his job and forces his fiancée Colleen to leave him. Unemployed and emotionally vulnerable, John eagerly takes what he thinks is the job opportunity of a lifetime as CEO of Morris Phillips. Distracted by his new high-powered job and its many duties, he has no idea that Lucifer secretly controls the multinational corporation or that his beautiful live-in assistant is a she-demon placed there to corrupt him. However as E'steem becomes romantically involved with John, she's torn between achieving her theocratic aspirations and saving the man she loves from eternal damnation.

Isis: Amari's Revenge
ISBN: 978-1481100670
Art Attack! Isis comes face-to-face with danger when a statue of Queen Amari comes to life on the floor of the Metropolitan Museum of Art. Returned to life through a magic spell, Amari seeks revenge on the woman she believes stole the heart of her Prince and her kingdom two thousand years ago.
As Isis works with her estranged sister E'steem, she seeks to extend an olive branch to the bitter Queen. Will she forgive and forget? Or will she continue to hold onto her two thousand year old grudge and finally mete out her vengeance on the goddess of retribution?

Isis: The Ultimate Fight
ISBN: 987-1481025874

Girlfight! Nemesis, the undisputed Queen of the Octagon is hungry for competition. After defeating twenty-four of the world's best MMA fighters, she's out to prove to both man and god that she's the best in the world. Traveling to the Island of Solitude she issues a challenge to the goddess Isis to fight her in the eight-sided chain-link roofed steel cage where the only way to win is to knock your opponent out. It's a war of the gods as New Heliopolis' Sword of Nubia takes on the Greek goddess of Retribution in a no holds barred brawl for it all.

Isis: The Beauty Myth
Myth ISBN: 978-1482309331

Glamorous! Raheema Sanders, 85-year-old CEO of Sepia Cosmetics seeks to find a way to reverse the effects of aging on herself. Learning that Isis is more than human, she has the goddess kidnapped and taken to her secret lab so she can learn the beauty secrets of the gods. However, when she comes face-to-face with the goddess she soon learns Isis' beauty is more than skin deep.

Isis: Death of a Theta
Kindle Exclusive

Requiem. In this flashback story set in 1973, Isis is called to the Theta House by her sorority sisters who want her to step down from her leadership role the Senior Grand Mother. With her mortal alias Andrea Robinson being 98-years-old, and Isis being immortal, they fear that if she continues on with the organization her secret may be revealed, and their mission compromised in the Black community.

Coming to terms with her aging secret identity, Isis realizes that she has to start making plans to get her human affairs in order. As she lays down her life of her alias in the mortal world for her friends, Isis comes to realize that she has to have faith in the women she taught to build on the foundation she established and pass it on to the next generation of Theta sisters.

Isis: My Sister, My Frenemy
ISBN: 978-1492308836
Frenemies! Things come to a head as Isis tells her estranged sister E'steem she still doesn't trust her. But when E'steem is kidnapped by the demon D'lilah, Isis realizes that she has to move their relationship past the frenemy zone to save her former arch-enemy from a fate worse than death.

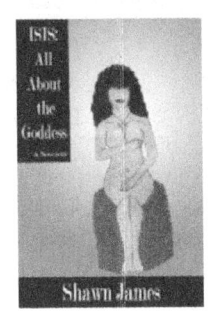

Isis: All About the Goddess
ISBN: 978-1492308256
Action! After someone makes a threat on the life of current college student and former child star Marilyn Marie, Isis goes undercover as an Art Model at the Next School. While the goddess exposes herself to the student body in class, the she tries to sketch out the details that will allow her to solve the mystery behind the threatening messages.

Catch up on the Isis series in paperback or in eBook at your favorite online bookseller!

Made in the USA
Coppell, TX
15 September 2022